The news that they were almost there gave the tired hikers a burst of energy. Even Aaron found himself walking faster—especially since he wasn't having to carry anybody on his back. He was next-to-last in line, a few steps ahead of little Dante.

"Doing okay?" Aaron asked, glancing back over his shoulder. The boy's face was flushed, but he was still charging along.

"Yeah," Dante replied. "But I'm thirsty."

"Me too. Maybe we can get some water or something at the top."

"Good."

Aaron walked on, letting his mind wander. It was a pretty day for a hike, and the cool air felt just right. The trip back down would be a lot easier.

Behind him, Dante suddenly gasped. "There's a mountain lion!"

—from *Mountain Lion*

On cover: The real Aaron Hall from *Mountain Lion*

REAL KIDS REAL Adventures™

NUMBER 11

Mountain Lion
Lifesaver
Race for Rescue

True Stories by
Deborah Morris

**Adventure
Ink**

Dewey Decimal Classification: JSC
Subject Heading: Adventure and Adventures \
Lifesaving—Stories, Plots, etc.
ISBN 1-928591-06-X

Cover design by Doug Downey
Text design by Sheryl Mehary

An imprint of *BookPartners, Inc.*
P. O. Box 922
Wilsonville, Oregon 97070

Acknowledgments

*The following adults are hereby awarded
the honorary title of "Real Kid":*

*Karen Solem,
for being a fun and sassy literary agent.
Charleen Davis,
for her colorful advice about book covers.
Aileen Kirkham,
for being both a friend and a cheerleader.
Donna Miller,
for golden apples in silver settings. (Look it up!)
Doug Downey,
for never losing his twisted sense of humor.
Terry Morris,
for tattoing our wedding ring onto his finger.
David Snyder,
for setting me a bad example. (He's my brother.)*

Mountain Lion

The Aaron Hall Story

Above: Aaron Hall

Aaron Hall's heart thudded painfully against his ribs as he huddled in the corner of the dark basement. Smoke filled the air, making the dark seem even darker to the frightened seven-year-old. When something brushed his face he clawed frantically at his cheek. It was only a sticky spider web.

He was afraid of spiders, but he was more afraid of fire.

The house above him was in flames. A few minutes earlier, he had run down to the basement and hidden in the farthest corner. Now he was trapped!

I can't breathe, Aaron thought. He coughed, gagging on the smoke. The smell was making his head ache. He hugged his knees to his chest and buried his head in his arms, trying to breathe through his sleeve. This was like some kind of bad dream.

Something heavy thudded on the basement stairs above him. Aaron's head snapped up. As he looked around wildly, a giant figure loomed out of the smoke, swiveling its head back and forth as if to look around the basement. Aaron held his breath. It had no face, but he could hear its breathing all the way across the room. It sounded like Darth Vader: *shhhhhh-tschhhhh.... shhhhhh-tschhhhhh.*

Aaron pressed himself farther into the corner. Would it see him?

With a sudden movement, the figure rushed toward him. When it bent over him, Aaron went limp.

He was being moved. Aaron kept his eyes pressed shut and let his arms dangle limply to his sides. Something hard was digging painfully into his back, but he was careful not to move. The horrible breathing sound was now just inches from his face.

Then—all at once—he sensed a change in the air. The smoke smell disappeared, and warm sunlight hit his face. He cracked his eyes open a slit. He barely had time to catch a glimpse of blue sky before he was dumped none too gently on the ground.

"Hey!" he complained. "I'm just unconscious, not dead!"

Above him, a smiling group of firefighters burst into laughter. Bill Colwell, the firefighter in charge, quickly pulled Aaron to his feet and dusted him off. "Great job!" he said. "You make a perfect training dummy. Thanks for helping us out today."

Aaron grinned. "It was fun! Well, it was a little

scary in the basement, like hide-and-seek in the dark. But it was still fun. Can I do it again sometime?"

Bill smiled. "Sure, next time I have a group of rookie firefighters to train. In real fires, little kids sometimes get scared and hide from us, so I teach my guys to look in closets, under beds, and anywhere else a kid can fit. That's why I told you to hide like that."

Aaron watched with interest as his scary-looking "rescuer" pulled off his helmet and mask. He'd been wearing a respirator—a breathing mask hooked to an air tank on his back. That's what had made the loud Darth Vader breathing sound.

"Never thought a little kid could be so heavy!" the young firefighter said, running his fingers through his hair. "I could've sworn you were at least a hundred pounds."

Aaron giggled. "Not yet. But I eat a lot!"

The rural fire station in Missoula, Montana, was practically next door to Aaron's house. For almost as long as Aaron could remember, Bill Colwell had let him hang around the station, helping roll fire hoses and other little chores. But this was the first time he'd let Aaron help with a real training.

Aaron sniffed his sleeve. "That fake smoke smells just like burned marshmallows!" he said, wrinkling his nose. "It was giving me a headache."

Bill Colwell nodded. "It's not half as bad as real smoke, though. That'll do more than give you a headache…it'll kill you if you breathe enough of it.

That's why we use the respirators. And that's why my man here," he patted the shoulder of the young fire-fighter who was still peeling off his suit, "had to crawl up the stairs with you instead of just walking you out. He had a respirator, but you didn't. He had to keep you low, where the smoke wouldn't be so bad."

"Oh," Aaron said. "I wondered why he didn't just run out. I never thought of that." He looked over at Fire Station #4 where the big fire engines stood waiting. "I want to be a fireman when I grow up. This is so cool!"

His rescuer grinned. "It's not bad. How many jobs can you get where somebody actually pays you to ride around in a big truck and play with fire?"

"And don't forget—we save people too," another man chimed in. "Old ladies, little kids, cats, squirrels, you name it. We're a regular group of superheroes. Right guys?"

"Yeah, that's us," the others agreed. "Superman, Spiderman, and Batman all rolled into one."

Aaron looked around at them. It would be cool to be a firefighter. He pictured himself in full gear, battling his way through huge flames to save a kid who was really trapped. He could almost feel the heat against his face... .

The flames flickered, casting a red-orange glow against Aaron Hall's face. His eyes narrowed with deter-mination. He took a deep breath—and blew out all sixteen candles on his birthday cake.

His mom, dad, and little brother Nathan cheered. "Okay, that's enough family togetherness," Nathan said. He was a skinny thirteen-year-old with a well-worn baseball cap. "Can we eat the cake now?"

Susan Hall gave Nathan a motherly glare. "It's Aaron's birthday, so he gets to eat the first piece. Go ahead, Aaron."

Aaron and his mother both had brown hair and brown eyes, but at age sixteen he already towered over her by several inches. He patted the top of her head. "I don't know, Mom. I kind of hate to cut this *homemade* cake."

Bruce Hall chuckled, and Mrs. Hall switched her glare to him. Her husband and son might not look alike, but they had the same sense of humor. "I guess you can call it homemade if you think of the grocery story as your second home," she told Aaron. "Which makes sense considering how much you eat these days!"

Aaron laughed. His mom worked as a speech pathologist at the local hospital, so she didn't have much time to hang around the house and bake. Aaron didn't care; he liked store-bought cakes.

A few minutes later, between mouthfuls of cake, Aaron talked excitedly about his newest summer job. "It'll be cool to go to Takachsin Boy Scout Camp this year as a counselor instead of a camper. I'm glad Marshall Day Camp gave me the time off. Mike and I will be sharing a tent."

"Yeah, and I'll get to have the house to myself for two whole weeks!" Nathan said.

"Just stay out of my stuff, dork. If I come back and find out you've messed with my things I'll have to beat you up. Again."

"Right," Nathan scoffed. "Then I guess I'll have to toss ice water on you while you're in the shower again. Last time you squealed like a girl: Eeeeeeeeeee!" Nathan waved his hands in the air.

"Seems to me that you were the one squealing when I got you back. How'd it feel to snuggle down into a sleeping bag full of snow?"

Nathan's face darkened. "That wasn't fair. I got in trouble for throwing a little water on you in the shower, but Dad just laughed when you sabotaged my sleeping bag. It took me forever to get all the snow out, and it left my sleeping bag all wet."

"That's what you get for being such a pain," Aaron said smugly. "Little kids bug me."

Takachsin Boy Scout Camp

The sun was low in the sky, dipping behind the jagged mountain peaks. Inside the camp dining hall, Aaron was busy working with a group of other staffers. He didn't look up when Shawn and Adrian, both staffers, hurried in. They went to sit at a long table with several of the older counselors.

A moment later, laughter broke out at the other table. Aaron twisted around in his seat to see what was going on.

Shawn was half angry and half laughing. "It's not funny!" he exclaimed. "If you'd seen how big that moose cow was you'd have been scared too." A female moose is called a "cow," and moose babies are called "calves."

Adrian nodded. "We were just walking along the crick bottom talking when *bam!* The calf was right in front of us. Before we could even turn around the cow snorted and started chasing us. We had to climb a tree."

That triggered another gale of laughter. Aaron grinned. "Hey, you guys! You actually let a mama moose tree you? I'd like to have seen that!"

Shawn gave Aaron a look. "I guess *you'd* have just stood there and tried to reason with her," he said sarcastically. "She would've bitten and trampled you soooo fast!"

"She was huge," Adrian said fervently. "Have you ever seen a moose up close? They're like elephants!"

Aaron shook his head. He'd never had a close encounter with a mama moose, but in his neighborhood, black bears sometimes wandered close to the houses. He'd never forget the night a mama bear charged the fence while he was in the backyard playing with his dog, Charlie. He never even saw the bear until she hit the back fence like a roaring freight train. Within seconds she scrambled over it and charged toward them. She must have had cubs nearby.

In a blind panic, Aaron turned and ran for the house, forgetting all about poor Charlie. It wasn't until he had darted inside and slammed the door behind him that he remembered the dog.

Fortunately, Charlie had also made a cowardly dash for the door and had somehow managed to crowd inside with Aaron. Aaron sighed with relief as he hugged Charlie hard enough to make him choke. They might both be cowards, but at least they were both alive!

Now Aaron smiled over at Shawn and Adrian. "I'm just kidding, you guys. Believe me, if I'd been there I would've been the first one up a tree."

The Wiener Mobile Patrol slowly lined up for breakfast, most stifling yawns. The Takachsin Boy Scout Camp had chosen a car theme that year, so the campers and staff were told to pick car-related names for their patrols, or groups. The campers had all picked boring patrol names like "Jaguar" and "Corvette," but the staff's decision had been unanimous. They would be the Wiener Mobile Patrol!

Aaron and his fellow staffers had gotten into the spirit by decorating the entrance to their camping area with a Wiener Mobile sign—a huge painted board with wheels tied to it. One of the older counselors had given them little red Wiener Whistles to wear on cords around their necks.

Joe, a second-year staffer, joined Aaron in the breakfast line. "Hey," he said with a tired grin. "You gonna make it today?"

"I guess," Aaron replied, covering a yawn. "I hope the kids take it easy on me today. I need a nap." The staff had stayed up late the night before, laughing and talking around the campfire.

Joe laughed. "Good luck. Were you here last year?"

"I was here, but just as a camper. This is my first year as a counselor."

"Oh. Well, were you around when that kid fell off the cable swing deal? He broke his shoulder or collarbone or something. It was bad."

Aaron thought. "I didn't see it happen, but I remember hearing something about it. Was he one of your kids last year?" That would be bad, having one of the campers in your group get hurt.

"No, but I was right there when it happened." Joe shook his head ruefully. "A bunch of us on staff were watching everybody take turns on the cable swing when that one kid slipped. He fell something like forty feet. We all just freaked out for a minute and froze. I felt really bad later."

This was the first Aaron had heard about the staff's reaction the year before. It was eye-opening to go from being a camper to being a counselor. You got to hear the inside story!

"So what did you do?" Aaron asked curiously.

"Once we all snapped out of it, we did okay. We called an ambulance and took care of him until it got here. It was just embarrassing that we didn't perform better in an emergency. I mean, that's part of what we're supposed to be teaching the kids, right?"

Aaron smiled. "I wouldn't worry about it. I'll bet the next time there's an emergency you'll be the first one to leap into action."

"Uh-uh. If we have any emergencies like that this year, they're all yours." He slapped Aaron on the back. "You new counselors need the experience."

Aaron stared into the flickering campfire, almost too tired to blink. He'd survived another day of hiking, games and teaching. Tonight he was going to get some sleep!

He was trying to work up the energy to crawl over to his tent when a twig snapped loudly on the dark mountainside above, sounding like a pistol shot. Aaron peered into the darkness, wondering what was moving around among the trees. It would take something pretty heavy to snap a twig like that.

Mike was sitting across the fire. "Did you hear that?" he whispered.

"Yep." Aaron was wide awake now. "What do you think it is?"

"I dunno. Why don't you get out your searchlight? Maybe we can nail it!"

Aaron scrambled over to the tent and pulled out the huge flashlight he'd brought from home. He clicked it on, then aimed it toward the spot where they'd heard the noises. The piercing beam revealed not one, but two furtive figures stalking their camp. Both were human.

Aaron pointed at the two giggling campers who'd been sneaking up on them. "Let's get 'em!" he yelled to the rest of the staff.

The two fastest staffers leaped up and started up the mountain after the boys. Aaron kept the searchlight trained on their friends as they chased the spying little campers all over the mountain. Nobody messed with the Wiener Mobile Patrol and got away with it!

By the time the spies were caught and hauled back to their own tents, it was once again well past midnight. Aaron groaned as he dragged himself into his sleeping bag and buried his face in his pillow.

Getting up in the morning wasn't going to be much fun.

Marshall Mountain Day Camp

"Kids!" Aaron exclaimed, stomping in the door after a long day at camp. "You wouldn't believe how some of these nine- and ten-year-olds act!"

His mother looked amused. "I raised a couple nine- and ten-year-old boys not too long ago. I think I'd believe it." She patted him on the shoulder. "Hard day at camp today?"

"Yeah. I'm just glad this session's almost over...the kids are all getting tired and cranky." He made a face. "At least I don't have the twelve- and thirteen-year-olds. They're seriously obnoxious."

"Hey!" Nathan said indignantly. He'd walked into the kitchen just in time to hear the last part.

"I wasn't talking about you, dork. Although now that you mention it... ." Aaron wasn't about to tell his little brother that the thirteen-year-olds at camp made him look good. He'd just get a big head.

By now Aaron felt like a seasoned camp counselor. He'd made it through the two-week Boy Scout camp with no disasters, and now he was back at Marshall Mountain Day Camp. Many of the kids at Marshall Mountain were first-time campers, so they needed to be babied a lot more than the Boy Scouts.

At least I get to come home every night and sleep in my own bed, Aaron thought wearily. He was still recovering from the late nights at Takaschin.

He took a quick shower, then decided to head into town to hang out with friends. As he backed his mom's Isuzu Trooper out of the driveway, he spotted Bill Colwell down the street at the fire station. Bill had been transferred to the main Missoula station and promoted to Lieutenant, but he came back to Station #4 now and then to help out.

Aaron waved as he drove past. Lt. Colwell waved back. Aaron had outgrown his dreams of becoming a fireman, but he still liked to watch the fire guys work. They had an exciting job.

Last Day of Camp

It was Friday, the last day of camp. The four staffers—Teresa, Julie, Shelley and Aaron—planned to finish off the week-long session by taking all thirty young campers on a day hike up Marshall Mountain.

"Most of these kids have never been on a hike in their lives," said Teresa doubtfully. "I'm not sure the younger ones will make it all the way to the top."

The three women counselors were all adults. Aaron was the baby of the group.

Aaron thought. "Okay, why don't we try this? About halfway up we can split forces. One of you can take the little kids back down, and the rest of us can take the more energetic ones to the top."

The women exchanged glances. Julie said, "I'll take the little kids back down when they get tired. Most of them are in my group anyway." She was in charge of the six- to eight-year-olds.

The mountain air was cool as they herded the excited campers into a wiggly line, the oldest kids at the front. The counselors spread out. Aaron went to the end of the line where he could keep an eye on the little kids. After working all week with nine- and ten-year-olds, the youngest campers looked tiny.

"Let's go!" Teresa called. With a cheer, they started up the trail.

Aaron liked being outdoors. As they moved up the mountain, he smiled at the efforts of a blond boy in front of him. He was the smallest camper in line, but he seemed determined to keep up with the bigger kids.

Aaron walked up beside up and tapped his shoulder. "Hey, what's your name?"

The boy looked up, his clear green eyes fringed with white-blond lashes. "I'm Dante Swallow," he said breathlessly.

"How old are you?" Aaron asked. The top of Dante's head only reached Aaron's waist. He couldn't be older than five or six.

"I'm six."

"Oh. Well, that's good." Aaron vaguely remembered seeing Dante around camp that week, mostly during the morning free times. He wasn't one of the troublemakers or whiners. Nice little kid.

Dante Swallow

They walked in silence for a few minutes as the trail snaked through thick trees, pine needles and twigs crunching under their feet. "How far is it to the top?" Dante finally asked.

Aaron shrugged. "I dunno. Are you getting tired?"

The little boy looked offended. "No, I was just wondering." As if to prove his point he sped up, leaving Aaron behind. Aaron smiled. The kid was tough!

After the first hour, though, Dante and some of the other younger campers were lagging behind. The older kids at the front would race up the trail, then stop to give the rest of the column a chance to catch up. Aaron stayed at the back, encouraging the stragglers.

One little boy finally sat down on the trail and refused to budge. "I'm tired!" he whined. "I don't want to hike any more!"

Aaron nudged him with his boot. "C'mon, you can do it. We'll be turning around soon, then you'll be walking downhill. It'll be easy."

The boy had picked up a couple sticks along the way, and now he was using them to stir the dirt on the trail. "No," he said stubbornly.

Aaron snatched the sticks from his hand and held them high, out of the boy's reach. "If you'll run all the way up to that next corner, I'll give you back your sticks. Okay?"

The boy gave him a sulky look. "I guess." He trotted unhappily to the next bend in the trail, where the end of the column was at least still in sight. Aaron handed him back his sticks. The boy promptly sat back down.

"Hey, knock it off!" Aaron said angrily. "If you think I'm going to carry you the whole way, you're crazy."

The boy looked at him defiantly. "Great," Aaron muttered. "This is just great." With a sigh, he grabbed the boy under his armpits to lift him to his feet. "We have to keep going," he said firmly. "I'll carry you for a little way, but that's it. Understand?"

"All right!" Quick as a monkey, the boy scrambled up onto Aaron's back, wrapping his arms in a chokehold around Aaron's neck. "Let's go!"

It's a good thing this is the last day, Aaron thought darkly as he started up the trail again, leaning forward to balance the extra weight. If I had to put up with much more of this, I might be tempted to leave this kid out here.

"Teresa! Julie! Aren't we at the turnaround point yet?"

Over two hours into the hike, Aaron felt like he'd already carried half the group at least part of the way. Only little Dante Swallow had steadfastly refused to be carried.

"I can do it," he said with dignity when Aaron finally asked if he needed a rest. The littlest kid in the group, and he was too proud to wimp out. Aaron wished some of the bigger kids would take notes from him.

Teresa dropped back to talk to Aaron. "The front of the column is already at the top. We might as well keep going now. The kids can all rest at the top."

The news that they were almost there gave the tired hikers a burst of energy. Even Aaron found himself walking faster—especially since he wasn't having to carry anybody on his back. He was next-to-last in line, a few steps ahead of little Dante.

"Doing okay?" Aaron asked, glancing back over his shoulder. The boy's face was flushed, but he was still charging along.

"Yeah," Dante replied. "But I'm thirsty."

"Me too. Maybe we can get some water or something at the top."

"Good."

Aaron walked on, letting his mind wander. It was a pretty day for a hike, and the cool air felt just right. The trip back down would be a lot easier.

Behind him, Dante suddenly gasped. "There's a mountain lion!"

Out of Nowhere

The words seemed to hit Aaron's ears in slow motion. He whirled around to see the hind legs and long tail of something big as it jumped from the thick brush along the trail...and landed on Dante.

Dante's terrified scream froze Aaron's blood. As Aaron watched, horrified, the animal pushed Dante over and pinned him to the ground, its front paws on his shoulders. Ears back, teeth bared in a fierce snarl, the mountain lion then turned its head to stare straight at Aaron.

Time stood still as Aaron's eyes locked with the animal's. It was easy to read the warning in the lion's eyes— *Stay back, or I'll come after you, too.*

In that instant, a hundred thoughts crashed into Aaron's head. He remembered his blind panic the time he faced the black bear—and abandoned his dog. He remembered years of Boy Scout lessons about being prepared. And he remembered Joe's story about how the staff froze the year before when the camper got hurt.

I can't freeze, he thought. I've got to do something.

The thought jolted Aaron into action. "Yaaaaah!" he yelled, stepping toward the lion and kicking dirt toward its face. "Yaaaaah! Get away from him!"

The lion didn't even flinch. Instead, it turned to sink its teeth into Dante's throat. The little boy's choked screams grew louder as he twisted to get away.

Aaron didn't hesitate. He ran up and kicked the lion on its side as hard as he could. "Let him go!" he screamed. "Yaaaaah! Let him go!"

The animal ignored him. Getting a better grip on Dante's throat, it picked him up and started dragging him off.

Aaron thought clearly, If I don't stop him now, he's going to kill Dante. He ran forward and aimed a hard kick at the lion's head. Angry, it twisted around to look at Aaron, its golden eyes fixed on his face. Aaron felt a thrill of fear. It didn't scare easily.

He kicked the lion's head again, then got right in its face. "Let him go!" he screamed. "Drop him!" Its teeth looked huge, especially from just inches away. It could take his arm off with one snap.

The cat was furious. After two more hard kicks to the head, it finally dropped Dante and backed off—but only about ten feet. Ears back, eyes murderous, it stood and stared at Aaron. Aaron waved his arms and screamed, afraid it was just waiting for a chance to pounce again. Finally, the cat vanished into the brush along the path.

Keeping one eye on the brush, Aaron scooped up Dante. The little boy was awake, but silent. Dead pale, his blond hair and shirt soaked with blood, he stared up mutely at Aaron.

"You're okay now," Aaron said. "I've got you." He shot another glance at the spot where the lion had disappeared, then ran a short way up the trail. Most of the kids were still hiking along, unaware of what had happened.

"All you kids get to the top, fast!" Aaron yelled. "There's a mountain lion back here!" His words caused a panic as the young campers screamed and stampeded up the path.

Aaron looked back down at Dante. There were several deep punctures on the boy's neck. He needed to stop the bleeding. "Hang in there, big guy," he said soothingly. "Everything's okay now." Still trotting up the trail, he put one hand over the worst wounds and pressed. Despite his confident words Aaron peered behind him fearfully. The cat was still out there somewhere. He could almost feel its eyes on his back.

A moment later he heard something moving fast, crunching down the trail in front of him. He was relieved when Teresa appeared.

"Oh my gosh!" she cried when she saw Dante. "What happened?"

"A mountain lion," Aaron replied briefly. "He's bleeding pretty bad. Do you have something we can use for a pressure pad?"

Teresa burst into tears. "Oh no," she moaned. She glanced around wildly. "Is it gone?"

Aaron decided there was no sense in frightening her. "Yes! Now get me something for a pad!"

Teresa pulled a piece of cloth out of her fanny pack. Aaron wadded it up and pressed it on Dante's neck. The boy didn't seem to be injured anywhere else. Aaron tried to keep his voice calm as he said, "Okay, Dante? I'm going to carry you up to the top. I know you didn't want to be carried, but that's too bad."

His attempt at humor didn't provoke a response. Exchanging a worried look with Teresa, Aaron ran faster up the path with the boy clutched to his chest.

It only took a couple minutes to reach the top. The news about the mountain lion had rocketed through the crowd of campers. Everybody was yelling and screaming. As Aaron panted to a stop, a maintenance truck pulled into the clearing along the service road.

Relieved, Aaron ran over and jumped into the passenger seat, still holding Dante. "Get us down to a hospital!" he gasped to the man behind the wheel. "A mountain lion got him!"

To his astonishment, the man jumped out of the truck. "Where'd it go?" he asked. The man turned back long enough to grab a gun from behind the seat. "Where'd the lion go?"

"Forget the lion!" Aaron yelled. "We need to get this kid to the hospital!" But by then the man was already running toward the trail.

Aaron once again found himself frozen. What should he do now? Then he saw the keys dangling from the ignition. He slid over into the driver's seat, still holding Dante.

"I'm taking your truck!" he yelled, not waiting to see if the man heard. He slammed the door and turned the key. He had just put it in gear when Teresa ran up and jerked open the passenger door.

"I'm coming too!" she shouted. "Don't leave me!"

Once she was inside, Aaron handed Dante over to her. "Come on, big guy, stay awake," he said roughly. Aaron shifted his gaze to Teresa. "Keep talking to him. He's pretty out of it."

Turning the truck, Aaron started down the dirt road as fast as he could. When they skidded around the first sharp curve, Teresa shrieked, "Slow down!" She was clutching Dante in one arm and holding onto the door handle with the other. The truck was bouncing pretty hard on the rough road.

Aaron was too stressed out to put up with driving instructions. "Get yourself together," he snapped. "We have to get help for this kid fast!"

"It won't help him if we crash!" she snapped back.

They were about halfway down the mountain when Aaron spotted a fire truck, lights flashing, coming to meet them. Someone at the top must have radioed for help. He pulled over and jumped out. To his surprise, Bill Colwell jumped out of the fire truck.

"Hi, Aaron!" Lt. Colwell called as he ran over to check on Dante.

"Hi, Bill." Aaron was too numb to think of anything else to say. An ambulance pulled up, and paramedics got out. As they loaded Dante into the ambulance, he finally started to cry.

"I'm going with him," Teresa said. She looked almost as pale as Dante.

Aaron nodded, a lump in his throat. "I'll go back up to check on the other kids. That lion's out of control."

Aaron watched the ambulance leave, then climbed back into the pickup truck, feeling like an old man. He steered the truck back up the mountain, hot tears spilling down his cheeks and dripping onto his shirt.

Camp was over.

From Practice Dummy to Hero

That night, Lt. Colwell came over to visit Aaron.

"I didn't hear all the details until this afternoon," he said as they sat at the kitchen table. "When I got the call this morning it just said that a camper had been injured, and that an employee was transporting the patient down the mountain. I was surprised to see you on the road, but I was *really* surprised when I found out what you'd done!"

Aaron grinned in embarrassment. "He was a tiny kid. I couldn't just stand there and let him get killed." He shook his head. "Is Dante really going to be okay? I heard he was released from the hospital this afternoon."

"I imagine he'll be fine. Little kids heal fast." Lt. Colwell smiled at Aaron. "You know, what you did today was really brave. Did you ever think you'd go from being a fire practice dummy to being a real hero?"

Aaron laughed. "Never crossed my mind."

Dante Swallow was treated at the hospital and released after getting almost forty stitches in his neck. Within weeks, he was back in the woods hiking and camping with his family.

The maintenance man with the gun shot and wounded the mountain lion when he caught it coming back up the trail toward the kids. Tracking dogs were brought in, and the lion was treed and killed.

For his role in saving Dante Swallow's life, Aaron Hall received the Boy Scout Honor Medal with Crossed Palms, the Carnegie Award for Heroism, and other awards.

Aaron Hall and Dante Swallow holding award certificates

Lifesaver

The Stephanie Shearman Story

Above: Stephanie Shearman

T he two seventh-grade girls stood behind Stephanie Shearman, laughing and whispering. Stephanie tried to ignore them as she sat outside the gym waiting for her mom to pick her up, but it was hard. They *wanted* her to hear their rude comments and mean laughter.

"She's so weird!" Amanda sneered. "Did you hear her accent?"

"Yeah. And she's from PAN-ama, wherever that is," Melissa replied. "She should've stayed there where she belonged."

Amanda and Melissa,* two of the most popular girls at Valley View Junior High, had stared at Stephanie from the moment she'd walked into the school gym that afternoon. Stephanie had seen them whispering as she introduced herself to several of the other girls on the

* Names changed

29

volleyball team, but she'd thought they might just be curious. Some of the others had asked a lot of questions about Panama. Most of them hadn't known it was a country.

Before long, though, it was clear that the two popular girls were jealous of the attention the new girl was getting. They'd done everything but throw rocks at her to show that she wasn't welcome.

Come on, Mom, Stephanie silently begged. Get me out of here. After living in Jonesboro, Arkansas for less than a month, she already hated it.

When the first piece of gravel hit her shoulder, she thought it was an accident—until she turned around to see Amanda and Melissa snickering. The moment she turned her back, she was showered with gravel. She couldn't believe it. They were actually throwing *rocks* at her!

Stephanie pressed her lips together. She felt like shrieking at them, maybe getting into a gravel war, but Amanda and Melissa were both twice her size. At age twelve, Stephanie weighed barely 60 pounds. The other girls could easily stomp her.

What's wrong with these people? Stephanie thought. I didn't do anything to them. She scanned the street, hoping she'd see her mother's Nissan minivan turning in. No luck.

Behind her, Amanda and Melissa were whispering again. Stephanie braced herself. What now?

To her surprise, they started singing loudly to the

tune of "Oh Christmas Tree," only the words were "Oh Pan-a-ma, oh Pan-a-ma! Why don't you go back the-ere!"

Stephanie felt tears welling in her eyes. Why did they have to be so mean? It was hard enough changing schools, much less changing countries. Careful to keep her back to her tormentors, she stood up and walked slowly toward the main school building. She could still hear them singing as she rounded the corner.

If it were up to her, she'd be on the next plane back to Panama.

I Hate This Place!

"Mom, it was awful!" she sobbed once she was safely in the car. "I hate this school! I hate this whole place!"

Pam Shearman looked stricken. "Calm down, baby. What on earth happened?"

Sniffling, Stephanie told her about Amanda and Melissa, and the rocks and the singing. Mrs. Shearman listened, her brown eyes wide.

"They actually threw gravel at you?" she asked. "Did they hurt you?"

"No," Stephanie admitted shakily. "It's not that. It's just—I don't fit in here! These girls have lived here all their lives. They've known each other since kindergarten. They don't want me here."

"I'm sure that's not true. At least," Mrs. Shearman added truthfully, "not for *all* of them. Didn't you meet even one nice person?"

Stephanie thought. "Well...there was this girl named Kelly. She came up when I first got there and started talking to me. I don't think she's in the group that hangs around with Amanda and Melissa."

"See?" said Mrs. Shearman with cheerful mother-logic. "Those two mean girls were just jealous. They'll get over it. Other than that, how was practice?"

Stephanie stared at her mom in disbelief. Her first day at volleyball practice she had people throwing rocks at her, and her mom asked "other than that" how was practice? Suddenly, the whole situation struck her as funny. She dried her eyes on the back of her sleeve and grinned.

"Well, other than *that* I guess practice was okay. Miss Stacey is nice, and she worked with me some on my serve. I doubt if I'll ever be a superstar at volleyball, but it's fun."

Mrs. Shearman reached over and tickled Stephanie until she squirmed away, giggling. "Are you laughing at me, Neener-beaner?" she demanded. "You'd better watch it. I'm still bigger than you."

The nickname had started years before when Stephanie was a baby. She was born in Italy, and since "*nina*" meant "small" in Italian, she soon went from Stephanie to Stephanina to Nina to—when her mom was acting silly—Neener-beaner. Her father still called her Nina sometimes.

Now Mrs. Shearman went on as if nothing had happened. "So tell me more about—was it Kelly? The girl who was nice?"

Stephanie nodded, keeping an eye on her mom. She was bad about starting tickle wars when you least expected it. "She just said hi and told me her name, then she introduced me to a couple of other girls. It was funny, though; when they asked where we'd moved from and I said 'Panama,' they said 'Where?' So I said, 'You know, the country.' They still didn't get it, so I finally said, 'It's a country in Central America, where the Panama Canal is!' Some of them thought I was talking about Panama City in Florida."

Mrs. Shearman laughed. "Well, not many girls your age have traveled as much as you have. I know it's been hard on you and Andrew having to change schools and make new friends every time your father gets stationed somewhere new, but that's one good thing about being an Army brat. You get to see the world!"

"I guess," said Stephanie wistfully. "I just wish we could've skipped this part of the world."

Changing Countries, Changing Schools

The move to Jonesboro had been hard for the whole family. Even Master Sergeant Jeff Shearman, newly stationed as an ROTC instructor at Arkansas State University (ASU), was having a hard time adjusting to the more relaxed college schedule and attitudes. A former Airborne Infantryman, he was used to more discipline.

For Stephanie, the change was more personal. In Panama she lived in a close-knit military community in the middle of a country so poor that only rich people wore jeans. She had many friends—in fact, she was one of the most popular girls in her sixth grade class. If she wasn't swimming or practicing solos for church, she was busy with her Girl Scout troop or competing in races. She had run a 10K race in an hour at age eleven.

Panama was a wild and beautiful country filled with lush banana plants, mountainous volcanoes and warm-hearted people. In Jonesboro, it wasn't only the climate that was colder…it was the people.

The first day of school arrived all too soon. After two weeks of volleyball practice, Stephanie had a good idea about what to expect. Amanda and Melissa had made it clear that Stephanie wasn't welcome at Valley View Junior High and never would be.

At least I have choir first period, Stephanie thought as she pushed her way through the crowded halls. She loved to sing, and she knew she had a decent voice. Maybe she'd meet some other friends like Kelly. It would help to have at least a *few* friends in Jonesboro!

Kelly was already in the choir room when Stephanie walked in. "Hi!" Stephanie exclaimed. "I'm so glad you're here! I didn't know you were taking choir."

"April and Miranda are here too," Kelly replied cheerfully. Those were two other girls from volleyball who'd been friendly. Stephanie started to relax. Maybe this school year would turn out okay after all.

"Well, if it isn't Miss Panama," said a familiar voice. With a sinking heart, Stephanie turned to find Amanda standing behind her. As always, Melissa was nearby.

So much for choir, thought Stephanie in dismay. She went to the other side of the room and sat down, wishing she could disappear.

Mrs. Ward, the choir director, introduced herself. "I'm going to go around the room and find out what part everyone's used to singing. When I call out your name, speak up. If you're not sure what you sing just say so."

While she was waiting for her name to be called, Stephanie looked around. One of the first things she noticed was that almost all the other kids were wearing cowboy boots. She looked down at her sneakers mournfully. The first day of school, and she already stuck out. Still, why should she wear boots just because everybody else did?

Then there were other small things—the name on her jeans, the fact that she didn't wear makeup. Styles were a lot different in Jonesboro than they'd been in Panama.

"Stephanie Shearman?" Mrs. Ward called. When Stephanie raised her hand, the teacher asked, "What part do you sing?"

"First soprano." Stephanie was proud of her voice range. First sopranos sang the highest parts, and often got to sing solos.

"Great." Mrs. Ward made a mark on her sheet and moved on.

Stephanie spent most of that day watching and listening as she went to each class. After changing schools so many times, she had learned it was always best to wait a few days before deciding what groups to join. She was still confident, despite the way Amanda and Melissa had "welcomed" her, that she could quickly fit in and make new friends.

"So Stephanie, what are your plans for the weekend?" As usual, Mrs. Shearman was the one trying to start a conversation at the dinner table. Every Friday night she insisted that the whole family eat together. It was supposed to be a time when they could all bond.

"Kelly and I are going to see a movie or something, then she invited me over to her house." Stephanie was happy to have been invited somewhere. Almost a month had gone by, and Kelly was still one of her few friends at school. She tried not to think about it. It was depressing.

Sgt. Shearman looked up, his blue eyes vivid against his tanned face. "When will you be home?"

Stephanie returned his look with identical blue eyes. "I'm not sure. I might spend the night at Kelly's house."

"Don't you *know* whether you'll be spending the night?"

"Not really. It depends on what we feel like after the movie." And also, she added silently, on what Kelly's mom said when they asked her!

Her father wasn't pleased. "Seems to me you should be able to plan something better than that. What movie are you going to see?"

Here it comes, she thought. "We haven't decided yet, Dad. We're going to see what's playing, then pick one."

Her father frowned. "If you don't have a better plan than that, I think—"

"Jeff?" his wife interrupted. "I think it'll be okay. Kelly's been over here a couple times. She's a nice girl. I'm sure they'll be fine."

Stephanie pushed her food around with her fork. It was no wonder she was so skinny, when every family dinner ended up being an interrogation! She decided to change the subject.

"I want to change schools," she announced. "I hate it at Valley View. All the kids are mean to me. I feel like a freak!"

"I thought things were getting better," protested Mrs. Shearman.

"Well, they're not throwing rocks at me anymore, if that's what you mean." Stephanie glanced up in time to catch a questioning glance from her dad. "It's a long story, Dad. It happened before school started, while you were still off at camp with your cadets. No big deal."

"If people are throwing rocks at my daughter, I'd like to know about it. How did it happen?" He made it sound if she had somehow brought it on herself.

"It wasn't *my* fault! It was just because I was new." She quickly told him the story, then added, "I hate Valley View. I'm never going to have friends. I don't want to keep going there."

"Well, you have to."

"But..."

"We've been through this enough times before, Stephanie. It just takes a while to adjust to a new place."

"But..."

"No buts. You're what—twelve? Thirteen? You're old enough to deal with things like this. Grow up."

I guess that's that, Stephanie thought resentfully as she speared a nasty-looking green bean. Her brother shot her a sympathetic glance. Andrew, two years older, was having his own problems fitting in. He was going to Valley View too, but he wasn't any help. She never saw him at school, and if she did he'd probably pretend he didn't know her.

An awkward silence fell around the table.

Mrs. Shearman tried to smooth things over. "Why don't we call and find out about the Girl Scout troop at Valley View?" she suggested. "Maybe you can make some new friends there. Is Kelly a Scout?"

Stephanie shrugged. "We haven't talked about it."

"You'll feel better once you get involved in some

activities here," her mother said hopefully. "You were always so busy in Panama...."

Stephanie pushed her plate away. "Can I be excused?" When she was in a bad mood she liked to be alone. That should be easy in Jonesboro, she thought, since nobody but Kelly wanted to be her friend.

A Chance to Dance

"Your brother is sooooo cute," Kelly whispered as she helped Stephanie fix her hair. They'd been on the phone all day talking about what they were going to wear to the school dance that night. Kelly had come over to Stephanie's house to finish getting ready. It was the first dance of the year.

"Andrew? You've got to be kidding! *Your* brother is the cute one." They both started giggling. It was silly, but they'd ended up having crushes on each other's brothers. "At least you have a date for the dance."

"Marvin's nice, but Andrew's cuter. Here, let me tie your ribbon."

Stephanie's dress was blue, with a pink and white striped ribbon that tied in a bow. When both girls were ready, Kelly's mom drove them to the dance. Kelly was supposed to meet Marvin there.

"Have a nice time!" Mrs. Cunningham called as they got out of the car. The girls waved as she drove off, then hurried into the school. It was chilly outside.

Stephanie and Andrew

The cafeteria, decorated with colorful balloons and streamers, was already packed with people. A live band was playing on the stage.

"Guess we're fashionably late," Kelly said, raising her voice to be heard over the music. "Oh, there's Marvin!" She drifted off into the crowd, leaving Stephanie standing alone.

Stephanie glanced around the room, hoping to spot at least a couple friendly faces. It was only then that she realized almost everyone else was wearing jeans.

Oh, no, she thought, her cheeks burning. A few other girls were wearing dresses, but they weren't "party" dresses with ribbons and bows. Stephanie wanted to run back outside before anyone saw her. She must look like a freak.

Then she mentally shook herself. Unless she wanted to spend the whole night hiding in the girl's bathroom, she was going to have to face her classmates. Kelly had on a fancy dress, too, but she wasn't letting it bother her. So what if they were overdressed? They were here to have fun!

She walked over to the punch bowl, trying to work up the nerve to ask somebody to dance. After sipping punch and looking around for a while, she decided to take a chance. There was a cute guy standing by himself watching the dancers. Maybe he was lonely, too.

Here goes nothing, Stephanie thought as she walked up to him. "Hi," she said with a friendly smile. "I'm Stephanie. Do you want to dance?"

The boy stared at her, surprised. "I don't think so."

Stephanie felt the blood slowly drain from her face. Without a word, she turned and walked back toward the punch bowl. She was still standing there like a statue a moment later when Kelly bounced over with a smile.

"What's up? Isn't this great?" Kelly beamed at Marvin. He had turned out to be more fun than she'd thought. It took her a second to realize that Stephanie wasn't answering. "Steph? Are you okay?"

"No, I'm not okay," Stephanie said distinctly. "I think I might throw up. Or maybe dying would be better."

"What's the matter? Did something bad happen?"

"Yes. I moved to Jonesboro!" Stephanie's cheeks were flushed, and her blue eyes glinted with tears. "I just asked some guy to dance, and he said *no!* I've never been so embarrassed in my life."

"Wow, that's pretty bad." Kelly glanced back at Marvin. "You want to dance with Marvin? I was going to get some punch and sit down for a while."

Stephanie gave Kelly a weak smile. "Thanks a lot, Kelly, but I don't think so. Marvin's with you."

"No, I mean it! I mean—"

"I know what you mean. But I'm not really in the mood anymore to dance. You two go ahead."

Stephanie found a chair in a corner where she could wait for the dance to end.

Fall swept through Arkansas, leaving the air cold and the trees spangled with brightly colored leaves. By mid-October as Halloween approached Stephanie looked more and more ghost-like. Instead of running, swimming, and hanging out with friends as she'd done in Panama, she spent most of her time at home watching TV.

The only thing that made school bearable was choir. When she was singing, it was easy to forget everything else. She was one of the few seventh graders Mrs. Ward had selected to try out for the All-Region Choir that year. Auditions were coming up that Saturday.

That Friday night, the family-bonding dinner went even worse than usual.

"Stephanie, what time are you supposed to be at MacArthur tomorrow morning for the choir tryouts?" her mother asked.

"Between eight and nine o'clock."

"I was afraid of that. Tomorrow morning is the 5K run at ASU. Your father and I are both running. You'll have to go with me or I won't be able to get you back to the tryouts in time."

"Mo-om!" Stephanie exclaimed. "I need to spend the morning practicing! This is important!"

"I know it is, baby, but this can't be helped. Besides, it'll be fun! We always used to run together in Panama." She glanced over at her husband. "Your dad will be way up front with his cadets, so I won't have anybody to run with. You know how old and slow I am."

"Mom, you don't understand! I'm trying out for the *All-Region* Choir. It's incredible. If I make it—"

"Stephanie!" her father interrupted. "Your mother already said that she can't get you to tryouts on time unless you go. Now you can either go and run with her, or you can go and sit in the car. Either way, you're going."

"I'm not even registered for the race! Even if I win, I can't get a medal."

"This isn't about getting a medal. It's about seeing what you can do."

"Great," Stephanie mumbled. "I know what I *can't* do. I can't run a 5K race, then make it in the choir tryout."

Ready...Set...Go!

Stephanie set her alarm for 6 A.M. the next morning, hoping to get in some practice before leaving for the race. She used headphones as she walked around the house singing "Scarborough Fair" at the top of her lungs.

She was singing, "Parsley, sage, rosemary and thyme..." when her brother's voice broke through the music. She lifted one earpiece and yelled, "What?"

"Will you *please* be quiet? I'm trying to sleep!"

Stephanie felt like screaming. She wished *she* could still be sleeping. Here she had an important audition, and she was being kidnapped at the crack of dawn to run in a race she wasn't even registered for.

"Get over it, Andrew. I have to practice." She snapped the earpiece back down and sang even louder.

Stephanie sulked all the way to the ASU campus where the race was being held. The running track was a big, wobbly circle, so the starting point would also be the ending point. The race was to start at 7 A.M.

As they joined the crowd of runners milling around, Stephanie felt her spirits lift. She'd never admit it to her mom or dad, but she was almost glad to be there. Maybe running would help her relax later at the tryouts.

There were about one hundred people in the race, and another twenty-five there to watch. Stephanie felt a little silly getting in the starting position without a number on her back, but what did it matter? She was also the youngest runner.

Her dad was lined up with his cadets. Her mom was next to her, ready to go. Stephanie took a deep breath and waited.

"On your marks... get set... *go!*" The starting pistol cracked, and the race was on.

Sgt. Shearman and his ROTC cadets quickly thundered past the other runners to take the lead. "That's the last we'll see of them before the finish line," Mrs. Shearman said, puffing. "I know you didn't want to run today, but it's nice to have you here. It's lonely doing things by yourself."

Tell me about it, Stephanie thought grimly.

They ran, gradually settling into a comfortable pace. Although the air was cold, it didn't take long for them to warm up. By the time they reached the first checkpoint they were both hot and thirsty.

Volunteers were lined up holding out paper cups filled with water. Without slowing down, Stephanie grabbed a cup, drank it in one gulp, and tossed the cup onto the pavement. The volunteers at the checkpoint would sweep up all the paper cups after the race.

The track was pretty, winding around through the trees on the university campus. Stephanie concentrated on keeping her stride even, pacing herself against several other runners. The next time she looked up, her mother wasn't beside her.

"Mom?" Stephanie slowed down and looked behind her. Sure enough, her mother was way back there. Stephanie jogged in place to give her a chance to catch up.

"Sorry," Mrs Shearman panted. "I can't keep up with you. You're just as fast as ever!"

"And you're just as slow as ever!" Stephanie shot back. "C'mon, let's try not to come in last, at least."

By the time they passed the second checkpoint Mrs. Shearman had fallen behind again. This time, Stephanie kept going. She was starting to get into the race. She passed an older man who was running side-by-side with a blond girl in her twenties, both of them talking and laughing. They caught Stephanie's eye. Usually she saw two old people together or two young people together. It looked funny to see an older man and a younger girl like that.

The next time she slowed down to wait for her mom, the couple passed her. She glanced at them again. The man was tall with gray hair and glasses. He looked like he was in his fifties.

Maybe she's his daughter, Stephanie thought doubtfully. She wondered briefly where *her* father was. He had probably finished the race and decided to run it again just for the exercise!

"Hey, Mom!" she called. "You think you can run any slower? At this rate I'll never get to tryouts on time. It'll be lunchtime before we get back to the finish line."

"Okay, okay," her mother said breathlessly. "I'm coming."

Over the next few minutes, they criss-crossed the older man and blond girl several times. First Stephanie and her mom would be in front, then the other couple would pass them, then they'd pass *them* again.

When they hit a small hill, Mrs. Shearman fell back. Stephanie slowed down, which gave the other couple a chance to pass again. They trotted by, waving at a campus policeman who was blocking a side road for the race.

Mrs. Shearman motioned for Stephanie to go on. She was just passing the policeman when it happened. If she hadn't glanced over at the other couple at that moment, she would never have seen it.

One second the man was running, the next second he dropped, crumpling to the pavement without a sound. His glasses flew off, and he landed hard on his side. He didn't get up.

The blond girl spun around. "Dad? *Dad!*"

Stephanie, only a few steps behind, was already at his side. At first she thought the man had just tripped, but one glance told her it was much more serious. He was unconscious, his fists clenched, his whole body shaking. His face was quickly turning purple.

The blond girl ran back and kneeled beside her father. "Somebody help!" she screamed. "He's not breathing! Does anybody know CPR?"

Does Anybody Know CPR?

Stephanie looked around wildly. Several other runners had stopped, and the policeman was standing right there watching. Why wasn't he doing anything? Why weren't *any* of them doing anything?

"Please!" the blond girl sobbed. "Does anybody know CPR?"

"I do." Stephanie quickly got down on the pavement next to the man, ignoring the surprised looks.

What should she do first? She'd been trained in CPR in Panama, both with the Girl Scouts and the American Red Cross. If somebody wasn't conscious, the first thing you had to do was check their breathing.

Just then her mother ran up. "Stephanie!" she said sharply. "Let the officer handle this!"

"Mom, he's not *doing* anything!" The fallen man's face was now a deep purple-blue, his teeth clenched tight. "Help me get his mouth open. He's got to get air."

As Mrs. Shearman hesitated, a man stepped forward. "How can I help?"

"I need to get his mouth open so I can breathe for him," Stephanie explained gratefully. "I can't pry his teeth apart."

Her tone seemed to snap her mother out of it. "Maybe we can do it together." While they forced the man's mouth open, Stephanie lightly touched his neck to feel for a pulse. He had a heartbeat, but it was faint. Unless he got some air soon, his heart would also stop.

The minute the man's mouth was open enough to let in air, Stephanie tilted his head back and pinched his nose shut.

Here goes nothing, she thought as she took a deep breath.

Just like she'd practiced with the Red Cross CPR manikins, she opened her mouth wide and covered the man's mouth completely. Then she slowly exhaled into his mouth, watching his chest. When she saw it rise, she knew the air had gone into his lungs.

She sat up and took another deep breath, keeping the man's head tilted back and his nose pinched. One breath every five seconds, she told herself. Two, three, four.... She opened her mouth wide and gave another slow breath. When she sat up this time, she could see the difference in his face. The ugly purple color was already fading to a more normal skin color.

Stephanie was only vaguely aware of the commotion going on all around her. The policeman was talking on his radio. The blond girl, Colleen Baker, was sobbing hysterically, both hands to her face. She had told Mrs. Shearman that her mother and sister, Bonnie, were somewhere at the race. Mrs. Shearman had gone ahead to try to find them. The rest of the bystanders simply stared.

The man on the ground was Dr. John Baker, a professor at the university.

Stephanie paused to see if Dr. Baker had started breathing on his own. She could feel a faint, uneven pulse in his neck, but he still wasn't breathing. She went back to breathing for him.

She hardly noticed when the ambulance arrived. She jumped when someone tapped her shoulder. "Okay, you can move out of the way now." It was a paramedic. He gave her a funny look as she hastily backed away, surprised to find a twelve-year-old in charge.

Legs shaking, Stephanie stepped back and watched as the paramedics checked Dr. Baker's pulse, then pulled out a defibrillator—shock paddles. When the unconscious man's body jolted up off the ground, Stephanie felt sick. She turned away, not wanting to see any more.

She started running again toward the finish line.

"What happened?" "We saw the ambulance…is somebody hurt?" "I heard it was Dr. Baker." "Are you okay?"

Stephanie tried to wave away all the questions. It hadn't really hit her until she'd run several blocks. Now her stomach was churning, and she was crying too hard to talk.

"I just…just…." She didn't even know what she was trying to say. She ran on, half-blinded by tears. She just wanted to finish the race and go home.

She made it across the finish line. Still sobbing, she went over to sit on some steps and wait for her mom. To her surprise, her father came over a moment later and sat down beside her.

"Hey, Nina, what's the matter?" His voice was surprisingly gentle.

"I'm j-just upset, Dad," she said, her voice muffled in her arms. "That man—Dr. Baker—was dying, and nobody was doing anything, and I had to *breathe* for him..."

Sgt. Shearman put his arm around her. "Look, you did your best. I'm really, really proud of you." He paused, then added, "Nina, did I ever tell you about the time I had to breathe for a man?"

That got Stephanie's attention. Still sniffling, she said, "No. What happened?"

"Well, you were probably a tiny baby at the time. It was when I was stationed in Italy. I got off the bus one day and saw this big crowd in the street. That usually means someone's been hit by a car or something, so I ran over to see if I could help. Sure enough, a man was lying there on the road, and he wasn't breathing."

"So what did you do?"

Sgt. Shearman shrugged. "The same thing you did. I breathed for him until an ambulance got there. Then I went on to work." He gave her a quick squeeze. "Speaking of work, it's time for you to get to your choir tryouts. You'll be late if you don't hurry."

Stephanie stared at him. "Dad, I can't go sing now! I don't want to see anybody else. I want to go home!" She practically wailed the last few words.

"You can't go off and hide every time something upsets you. You've been practicing for this competition for months, and you need to see it through. Just put all this out of your mind for now."

The ride to MacArthur Jr. High passed in a blur. Stephanie was still crying when her mother pulled up in front of the school. "Come on, baby, you can do this." She gave Stephanie a big hug and kiss. "I love you, and good luck!"

I'll need it, Stephanie thought with a sinking heart as she walked into the gymnasium crowded with hundreds of competitors—almost all eighth and ninth graders.

Monday Morning

The first thing Stephanie saw when she got to school on Monday morning was a copy of the front-page newspaper story where her picture appeared under the blaring headline: LIFESAVER. The school counselor was running around showing everybody.

Oh, great, Stephanie thought gloomily as she slipped into the choir room a few minutes early. She could already hear the mocking comments Amanda and Melissa's crowd would make.

But at least Dr. Baker was going to be okay. No matter what else happened, Stephanie was glad she'd been able to help.

She was sitting quietly, lost in thought, when other students started filing in. She glanced up to see Heather and Ashleigh,* two of Amanda and Melissa's close friends, staring at her and whispering. She quickly looked away.

"Stephanie?"

Startled, Stephanie looked up a moment later to see the other two girls standing beside her. They both looked uncomfortable. What did *they* want?

"Hi," she said.

With a glance at Heather, Ashleigh said awkwardly, "Uh, we just wanted to say we thought it was cool what you did for that guy. You know, at the race."

Stephanie couldn't believe her ears. They were being *nice* to her! "Thanks," she replied. She didn't know what else to say.

"So where did you learn how to do that?" Heather asked. "I mean CPR and all that stuff."

"In Girl Scouts," Stephanie replied. "My troop in Panama took a Red Cross course so we could get our First Aid badges. I never thought I'd use it, though." She added honestly, "I was really scared."

Kelly and April joined them, and other students gradually drifted over. When Amanda and Melissa walked in together, they stopped in their tracks at the sight of the smiling group gathered around Stephanie.

"What's going on?" Amanda asked loudly. It was clear that she expected her followers to instantly run to her side. Instead, several of them just looked at her.

* Names changed

"Didn't you hear?" somebody asked. "Stephanie saved a guy's life this weekend. It's in all the papers."

Amanda's eyes narrowed. "Big deal," she said. "Come on, Melissa." They stalked across the room to their seats.

Just before the bell rang for class to start, Mrs. Ward posted the sheets giving the results of the All-Region Choir tryouts. Several students ran over to check for their names.

Kelly scanned the sheet, then looked up with a big grin. "Hey, Stephanie! You made alternate first soprano for All-Region!"

Stephanie grinned back. It looked like the move to Jonesboro had turned out to be a great idea after all.

Stephanie receiving Medal of Honor

Stephanie,

I wanted to take this opportunity to thank you and your family for your heroic actions. I am eturnally grateful to you. You gave my dad life. You placed his life above yours at that moment. You could have just as easily ran by, but you stopped. Thanks to you I have my dad.

My dad and I are extremely close. I can't imagine my life without him Thanks to you I don't have to.

You are such a strong young lady.

Continue to grow in all ways. I really admire your strength and courage. I am so thankful for you. Thank you for what you did.

Bonnie Baker

Letter from Bonnie Baker

Thanks to Stephanie's quick actions, Dr. John Baker, 52, made a full recovery. His daughter Bonnie crossed the finish line to place first in the overall women's division before learning of her father's collapse.

Stephanie Shearman received the Medal of Honor from the Girl Scouts of America, a Lifesaving Award from the Governor of Arkansas, and various other awards.

Race for Rescue

The Eli Goodner Story

Above: Eli Goodner

I n the early morning light, the sputtering flare looked like a stick of dynamite. Fifteen-year-old Eli Goodner hastily took aim and threw it toward the forty-foot pile of wood—the Wallace High School football team's homecoming bonfire.

The flare bounced off a log and landed upside down in the stack. It didn't seem to be doing much damage.

Eli's friend Chad was standing beside him. "Come on, come on," he said nervously. Since his well-known blue Ford truck was their getaway car, he wanted to get away before anybody saw it. The neighboring towns of Wallace and Kellogg, Idaho were both small.

After a long moment of suspense, the gasoline-drenched wood ignited with a loud *WHUFF!* Orange flames danced deep inside the woodpile.

"Yes!" Eli crowed. "We did it!" They watched for a second to make sure the flames wouldn't die out, then ran back to Chad's truck and threw themselves inside. The tires spurted gravel as they tore out of the parking lot.

The Wallace High School Miners and Kellogg High School Wildcats had enjoyed a fierce rivalry for years. Both prepared a homecoming bonfire every year, and students made a game of camping out overnight to guard their bonfires from being prematurely lit. They could count on at least one midnight raid every year by the other school.

Eli looked back. Black smoke was already belching high into the sky behind them, fanning out across the parking lot. He grinned with satisfaction. This year, the Kellogg Wildcats had won the Great BonfireWar!

"That was cool," Chad said, starting to relax now that they were on their way back to Kellogg High. "I guess this is the first time anybody's tried to torch the bonfire in the morning instead of at night."

"We're geniuses," Eli said modestly. "I wish I could see their faces when they find out. I think we're the first ones in, like, two or three years to actually torch a bonfire without getting caught." Eli settled back comfortably into the passenger seat. "What time is it?"

Chad glanced at his watch. "We've got about twenty minutes left till second period. Want to go get a cheeseburger or something? We need to air out. We still smell like gas."

"No, we'd better get inside. Maybe it doesn't count as skipping if you miss less than one period."

Eli and Chad had been friends since childhood. They had often been mistaken for twins—they were the same size, with blond hair and blue eyes. Oddly enough, both their dads had also worked as miners. Eli and Chad shared a locker at school and hunted and fished together, but this was their first outing as partners in crime.

Eli and Chad, age 13

Slipping into the school, Eli stuffed a few things into the locker, using one hand to keep it all from avalanching onto his and Chad's feet. "So who all are we going to tell?" he asked in a low voice. "We have to tell somebody, or what's the point?"

Chad shrugged. "As long as it doesn't get back to Mr. Dunn." Dunn was the vice principal at Kellogg High. He didn't have much of a sense of humor.

Eli was a little worried about Coach Amos finding out. Eli was receiver on the football team, and championships were still ahead. Coach might bench him for the rest of the season if he knew. Still, wrestling was coming up next, and Eli had about decided that he liked that better anyway. Everything would work out.

"See you later, Chad," he said. "I've got to get to Biology. Heather doesn't know anything about this morning. I'll tell her for sure!"

Like Chad, Heather had been a friend forever. Well, more like a girlfriend now that they were sophomores. She was beautiful—tall with long blond hair and soft brown eyes. She wore braces, but on her they looked like tooth jewelry. Eli had already decided he wanted to marry her once they graduated.

Heather flashed him a bright smile when he walked into class, but her smile quickly faded as he moved closer. "Eli, you smell like gas," she said, wrinkling her nose. "What did you do?"

Eli tried to look innocent, but it didn't work. Heather knew him too well.

"Umm...Chad and I skipped first period and lit Wallace's bonfire."

"What if you get caught?" she whispered fiercely. "You're going to get in trouble!"

"No way. No one was around to see us. They were all in class."

A few minutes later, in the middle of class, an office aide brought a note to Biology. The teacher glanced at it, then called Eli to the front. "This is for you," she said, handing him the note. "Mr. Dunn wants to see you in the office."

Eli's stomach sank. He glanced back at Heather, then followed the aide to the front office. How had they found out so fast? He tried desperately to think of some good excuses, but having just finished qualifying as an Eagle Scout he knew he couldn't lie. Still, why should he and Chad get in trouble for being loyal Wildcats?

Mr. Dunn was waiting, his face grim. This was looking worse and worse. "Into my office, if you please, Mr. Goodner."

Through the glass Eli could see Officer Spike, one of the police officers in Wallace's small force. Spike looked up with an insincere half-smile, and Eli's heart sank even lower. Just how much did they know? He sat down, trying to appear unconcerned.

Mr. Dunn cleared his throat. "So, Eli, what did you do this morning?"

Do the Crime, Do the Time

Eli was pacing back and forth in the kitchen while his father made breakfast.

"This is so stupid, Dad! After they hauled me up to the office, they laughed about it all and said it was no big deal. They said I might as well tell them all about it since they had two witnesses who saw us leave. Then when I did, they got all serious and said they'd call me later about the charges. I thought they were kidding, but this morning they called to say I'm being charged with *arson,* like some criminal or something."

Roy Goodner sighed, running a hand through his salt-and-pepper gray hair.

"Eli, I don't even know why I'm listening to this." His wheelchair wheels and silver-rimmed glasses both caught the early sunlight coming through the window, sending dots of light dancing around the kitchen. "That whole thing was incredibly dangerous. Do you have any idea what gasoline can do? Just the *fumes* can explode like dynamite! And then you light a *flare?* I thought you had better sense than that."

He rolled back to the stove to grab the pancakes that had just finished cooking, then paused to flip the omelet on the other burner. "You can get started on these pancakes if you want," he added, sliding them onto Eli's plate. Even when he was mad, he rarely lost his temper.

Eli took the pancakes over to the table. "They nailed Chad, too. He just finished telling his dad about it when the police showed up. Now we each have to pay $800 fines and do a hundred hours of community service! Plus we're both suspended for three days." Eli stabbed his pancakes fiercely. "It's not fair, Dad. We were just having fun!"

Roy Goodner swiveled his wheelchair around to face his son. "What kind of excuse is that? I thought I was just 'having fun' the night this happened." He nodded down at his paralyzed legs. "Maybe suspension and a fine is a cheap price to pay for a good lesson."

Eleven years before, when Eli was only four, Mr.Goodner had worked on the mining crew that sank the deepest shaft in North America. At the big celebration party afterward, he had too much to drink—and on his way home he lost control of his car and crashed. He woke up weeks later in the hospital, paralyzed from the waist down.

Now Eli looked down, ashamed. What could he say? His father almost never complained, but he knew the accident had changed his life forever.

Mr. Goodner went on, "Eli, you know in this family we respect the Lord and respect other people. You're just lucky that nobody got hurt this time. I want you to promise me that you won't pull a dumb stunt like this again."

Eli groaned. "Dad, why do you always have to make me promise stuff? You've already made me promise not to drink and drive, not to do drugs, to come home on time, to take care of different stuff…. Why do I always have to *promise?*"

His father smiled. "Because I know that promises work with you. Once you promise me something, you always do it. I don't have to think about it again. That's one of the most important things a man can have—faith in his word."

Eli grunted unhappily and stared at his half-eaten pancake.

"So, how about it?" his father prompted.

Eli put his fork down with a clatter. "Okay, okay, I promise. I won't do something this stupid again."

"Good." Mr. Goodner lifted the skillet, rolled over to the table, and slid the omelet onto Eli's plate. "Now finish your breakfast and get out of here. I have work to do." His smile told Eli that he'd already been forgiven.

A Hunting We Will Go

"Eli, hurry up! If you take much longer I'll be too old to go hunting!"

Roy Goodner had won a drawing that gave him a three-day permit to hunt in a special area reserved for disabled hunters. Each winning hunter was allowed to bring one other person with them. Roy had invited Eli.

Eli shuffled in, yawning. It was barely daybreak on Saturday morning. The temperature outside was supposed to drop to near zero that day. Eli was wearing a green wool overcoat and a bright orange hunter's cap.

"Do we need to pack sandwiches or anything?" he asked.

His father shook his head. "Nah. Let's just take some water and granola bars to snack on. We'll be home by one or two. We can get lunch then."

Sherrie Goodner walked in and kissed her husband on the top of his head. "I thought you boys were going somewhere. If you're going to hang around here all day I'll find some work you can do."

Mr. Goodner grinned and started rolling for the door. "I've been ready for an hour. It's our son who seems to be moving in slow motion this morning. C'mon, Eli, let's get out of here before your mom sticks us with chores!"

"I'm right behind you." Eli had a bottle of water tucked under one arm and some granola bars half-stuffed in his pockets.

Mrs. Goodner laughed. "I thought that might get you two moving. I wish I could go, but I have to deliver an order." Eli's parents ran a jewelry shop out of their home. For years—ever since Mr. Goodner's accident—they had worked side by side handcrafting jewelry from silver and gemstones mined from the area: Indian turquoise, garnet, moss agate, tiger's-eye, and others. You could tell they enjoyed life, and life together as well. They sold their jewelry to shops all over the country.

"We're outta here," Mr. Goodner said cheerfully, hitting the ramp leading from the porch down to the driveway. Eli had to trot to keep up with him.

Sherrie Goodner stepped out onto the porch to see them off, then shivered as the cold air hit her. "I'm going back inside. It's too cold to stand out here. Bye!"

"Bye, Mom!" Eli called. It was cold. He considered going back in for his gloves, then shrugged. He didn't mind cold weather, and this was just a road hunt, more of a scouting trip than anything else. Unless his dad shot something, he'd never leave the heated van.

Reaching the van, his father hit a switch on the side. A wheelchair lift—a moving platform like a small open elevator—slid out from the back doors and dropped smoothly to the ground. Mr. Goodner rolled onto the lift, then hit another switch that made it go back up. In seconds he was in the van, slamming the back doors and rolling toward the driver's seat.

It was easy now, after years of practice, for him to move from wheelchair to driver's seat, collapse the wheelchair, and slide it out of the way. With the help of the lift, he could be on the road about as quickly as any able-bodied person. Since he couldn't use his feet, the van had a special steering wheel with hand controls for the gas and brake pedals.

Eli climbed into the passenger seat while his dad slid a Christian music tape into the cassette player. Once they were on the road, music blaring, Eli leaned his head back against the seat and dozed off. It was way too early to be out of bed.

His father poked him awake forty-five minutes later. "Hey, sleepyhead! Hop out and open this gate for me, eh?" Eli sat up and looked around sleepily. They were stopped in front of a locked steel gate at the base of a mountain.

"It's locked," he said stupidly.

His father smiled and held up a key. "It came with my permit, remember? We'll have the whole place to ourselves!"

Still groggy, Eli took the key and swung open the passenger door. The blast of icy air woke him up in a hurry. He jumped down onto the snow-splotched ground and hurried over to unlock the gate.

"Come on!" he yelled, swinging the gate wide and motioning to his dad to drive through. He'd have to lock it again behind them.

By the time he climbed back into the van, Eli was shivering. "Man, it's cold out there!" he said, warming his hands in front of the van's heater. "Reminds me of the Freezeree campouts we used to have."

As they began the slow climb up the mountain, Eli's eyes once again grew heavy. Lulled by the music, rocked by the bumps in the dirt road, he soon drifted back to sleep.

He woke up with a start when the van jounced painfully over a low spot. Eli sat up and glanced out of the window, watching for a sign to see how far they'd come. He finally saw a mile marker that said: **3**.

I must not have been asleep long if we've only

come three miles, he thought. He looked around with interest. Now that they were inside the reserve, it was time to start watching for deer.

"You finally awake?" his father asked.

"Yeah…did you see anything interesting while I was asleep?"

"Oh sure. Two giant bears, a cougar, coupla bobcats, six mule deer, an elk…you know, the usual. Too bad you missed all the excitement."

"I'll bet," Eli said. "Did any of them resemble alderbrush by any chance?" Alderbrush was a thick cane-like weed that grew up to fifteen feet tall. It seemed to be clumped on every corner.

"Maybe," his father admitted. "Actually, they've kept the main road pretty clear of alders, but the side trails look choked. Good thing this van is so heavy…we'll be able to crunch right through it."

They slowly worked their way up the mountain, following the zig-zagging dirt road through the trees. Every now and then Eli caught a glimpse of the highway and frozen river far below. He sat up taller in his seat, straining to see down the steep slope. From this height, the river was only a tiny silver snake.

While Mr. Goodner concentrated on driving, Eli watched for promising hunting spots. Many game paths sprouted from the dirt road, so it was easy to imagine deer and other wild game hidden in the thick brush and among the pine trees. What a great place to hunt!

When Mr. Goodner finally stopped and pulled out his binoculars, Eli pointed out a well-used game trail off to one side. "What do you think about that one? It looks like there's been good hunting there in the past, anyway."

"Let's follow it a little way and check it out."

They bumped off the main road onto the narrow trail, which was partially blocked by alders. The van plowed on, pushing through the thick brush like an army tank. There was a steady thrumming sound as the plants whipped against the front and sides of the van.

They passed through several clearings before reaching a small, shady canyon. The temperature in the shade seemed to drop several degrees. Eli was grateful for the hot air blowing full blast from the vent. As much as he liked to hunt, he wouldn't want to spend a whole day out in this killer cold.

Roy Goodner also felt the drop in temperature—at least from his waist up. He suddenly wished Eli had worn hunting boots instead of thin tennis shoes. If they were lucky enough to bag a deer on their first day out, Eli would be the one to get out and retrieve it. Zero-degree weather can be dangerous if you aren't dressed for it.

As a paraplegic, Mr. Goodner always had to be extra careful about the cold. Since he couldn't feel his legs and feet, they could literally freeze—or burn—without him noticing. He'd never forget the time he bought expensive battery-operated socks to protect his feet from the cold, and ended up practically cooking them instead. He had to go to the hospital with third-degree foot burns. That was embarrassing!

Beside him, Eli stirred restlessly in his seat. "I haven't seen a single deer or anything else out here so far," he complained. "Are you sure there's game in here?"

"That's what I hear. Let's keep looking."

Their view of the trail ahead was blocked by another thick patch of alderbrush. Mr. Goodner nudged the van forward into it. They were about halfway through the alder patch when the engine sputtered and died.

Eli gave his dad a questioning look. "Uh, Dad, we're not out of gas or anything are we?"

Mr. Goodner rolled his eyes. "Very funny, Eli. No, we've got plenty of gas." He turned the key and the engine cranked, but didn't start. He tried again. Same result.

The music from the tape player suddenly seemed loud in the quiet of the frozen wilderness.

This Can't Be Happening

"Well, this is just great," Mr. Goodner said in disgust. He tried one more time just to make sure, but it still didn't start. Something was wrong with the van.

Eli looked around. They were literally stuck in the middle of a giant bush, branches pressed tightly against the windshield and all the windows. It would've been funny if they hadn't been out in the middle of nowhere.

"Let me take a look at the engine," Eli offered. "Maybe it's something simple like a loose wire or something," He grabbed the handle and tried to swing his door open, but the brush was too thick. He couldn't open the door.

"This is wild," Eli muttered. "I'll have to go out the side door."

He eased out of his seat and moved, hunched over, into the back of the van. Looking at the thick branches outside, he pulled a small hatchet from his backpack. He might have to hack his way out!

He rolled open the sliding door and eased out. The alders were not only thick, they were sharp! Eli started chopping.

"Be careful," Mr. Goodner cautioned. He tried again to start the van. Nothing.

By the time Eli cleared a small path to the front of the van and hacked away enough of the brush so he could open the hood, his hands were numb with cold and covered with scratches.

"Can you see anything?" his father asked.

Even with the hood open, it didn't help much. Eli wiggled all the wires and checked everything else he could reach. He couldn't find anything wrong.

"No," he said shortly. "Dad, there's no way. If anything in here is broken, I can't get to it." He slammed the hood and eased his way back around to the sliding door. By now, the inside of the van wasn't much warmer than the outside. Eli got in and closed the door anyway.

He and his father looked at each other, the same thoughts running through their heads. With the van broken down, they were stranded. Not only were they in a locked reserve where other people wouldn't be driving through, they were off the main road and surrounded by tall brush, almost invisible. The van's heater wouldn't work without the engine running, and the temperature outside was dropping fast.

"I can't believe this," muttered Mr. Goodner. "Come on, start!" He cranked the engine again, with the same discouraging result.

Then, as they watched in disbelief, snowflakes started filtering down through the alderbrush and sticking to the windshield. The first snowfall of the season, and it had to be today!

"Well, if we aren't home by dark your mother will come looking for us," Mr. Goodner said, trying to sound upbeat. It was close to noon.

"By then we'll both be popsicles. Trust me, it's cold out there!" Eli hesitated, then said, "Dad? I think I'd better go get us some help. I'm in great shape, the best I've ever been. I'll just run back and stop at the first house I see. I'll call Mom, and she can come get us. It'll be fine."

"Eli, it's a long way back."

"It's not that far," Eli said, remembering the three-mile marker they'd passed. "Three or four miles, right?"

"It's a lot farther than three miles! You slept most of the way in. Besides, I don't like the idea of you getting out in this cold. You're not dressed for it."

"Running will keep me warm. I'm a lot more worried about you. I could start a fire for you and put your chair next to it, but if it went out before I got back you'd be in trouble." Eli looked at him. "Come on, Dad, you know there's no other way. I have to go."

Mr. Goodner fell silent. He finally sighed and nodded. "I hate to admit it, but I guess you're right. Are you sure you know the way?"

Eli made an exasperated sound. "Dad, I'm fifteen, not five! I think I can follow the trail back to the main road without you holding my hand." He thought for a second. "I'll probably just cut down the slope to the highway. That'll save a lot of time."

"No!" Mr. Goodner's voice was almost a shout. "It's way too steep and slippery. If you fall and get hurt, we'll both freeze out here. I want you to stay on the main road, Eli."

"Give me a break! I'm not going to fall, Dad. It doesn't make sense to take the long way when there's a shortcut!"

"It makes sense to me," his father said firmly. "It's too dangerous for you to make that climb by yourself. Even if you didn't fall, you could be caught in a rock slide. They happen here all the time."

"Dad…"

"No, Eli! I'm not going to let you do that. It's a stupid idea." Mr. Goodner gave him a sharp look. "Promise me you won't."

Eli groaned. "Oh, come on with the promises already! I'm tired of promising things."

"Promise."

"Dad…"

"Promise me, Eli."

Eli finally gave in. "Okay, okay, I promise I won't take the shortcut."

Mr. Goodner eyed him. "Will you shake on it?" He stuck out his hand and waited. Eli reluctantly took it, knowing that to his father it was the ultimate pledge.

"Good. Now get going. We both need to be out of here by dark."

Before Eli left, he went through the van gathering up warm things to wrap around his father. There wasn't much—just a couple thin blankets and a big plastic tarp.

"This is all I could find," he said, tucking one blanket around his dad's shoulders and the other around his legs. "I'm going to put this tarp around you, too."

"I feel like a sausage," Mr. Goodner joked as Eli wrapped him in the plastic. About the only thing still showing was his face.

Eli looked at his handiwork critically, then peeled off his wool overcoat to add to the coverings. He kept on his flannel-lined windbreaker.

"Put your coat back on!" Mr. Goodner protested, trying to untangle his arms from the wrappings. "You're the one who'll be out in the cold. You can't go out there without a thick coat!"

"Listen, Dad, I'll be running the whole time. You'll have to sit here in one place. I don't want you to freeze."

"But I'll be out of the wind," his father argued. "*Please,* Eli."

"I'd have a hard time running in an overcoat anyway. It would flap against my knees the whole way. It'll do more good here."

Mr. Goodner didn't like it, but he saw that Eli was right. "Well, at least take the rifle with you. These woods are full of bears and cougars."

Eli grinned. "And supposedly deer, although I haven't seen a single one so far!" They both laughed. Eli put the water bottle and granola bars where his dad could reach them, then slung the rifle over one shoulder. He already had the gate key safely in his jeans pocket.

"I'll be back soon. Keep warm."

"I love you, Eli. Be careful."

Eli smiled. "Bye, Dad."

In an instant, Eli was out of the van and pushing his way through the alders. As soon as he hit the clearing, he began to run.

Please, God, take care of my dad, he prayed. *Keep him warm.*

The Longest Run

After the first thirty minutes, Eli settled into a steady pace. At first he used his hands to wipe away the wet snowflakes that hit his face, but now he just ignored them or blinked them away. His breath made a string of small puffs in the air. He soon tired of the rifle bumping against his back as he ran, so he started carrying it in his hands.

He hesitated when he reached the main dirt road. What if he had trouble finding the right turnoff when he came back? The trails all looked alike. He thought about using a bent branch or a pile of rocks as a marker, but decided they might disappear under a coating of snow. Instead, he pulled the orange hunter's cap from his head and stacked a few rocks on top to keep it from blowing away. Even coated with snow, he should be able to see that!

He started running again—this time toward the entrance gate.

Roy Goodner sat in the van, trying to distract himself by listening to tapes. Eli had been gone less than an hour, but he was already feeling the chill.

Mr. Goodner was worried, but not about freezing. The thought of Eli out there all alone, running through the frozen wilderness wearing only jeans and a wind-breaker, left him weak with fear.

Take care of my boy, he prayed. *Keep him warm.*

Eli's lungs felt like they were on fire. It seemed crazy that he could sweat while he was running through snow flurries, but it was happening. When he slowed down to catch his breath, the sweat on his skin turned icy cold. It was easier to just keep running.

He switched the rifle back and forth, sometimes keeping it slung over his back and other times holding it as he ran. He kept watching for the mile marker he'd seen on the way in. When he finally spotted the sign with the **3**, he felt a surge of relief. Only three more miles to the entrance gate!

"Almost there," he said aloud, wanting to break the snowy silence. He slowed to a walk to catch his breath—and that's when he noticed something odd about the mile marker. A faded **1** was barely visible next to the **3**.

Eli suddenly felt sick. The sign wasn't marking three miles. It was marking thirteen!

The shock left Eli numb, unable for a moment to think. It was impossible. He'd already been running for over an hour, and now he had another thirteen miles to go?

"I can't do this," he said, swatting angrily at the snow blowing into his face. "I can't do this!"

In the end, though, he didn't really have a choice. Knowing how much farther he had to go, every minute counted. This was now a race for his father's life.

He quickly calculated how long it would take him

to cover thirteen miles. On a level track he could easily jog six or seven miles per hour, but this wasn't a level track. The best speed he could hope for now was probably three or four miles per hour. He would barely make it out and back before dark.

Without thinking, he glanced over toward the slope, clearly visible through the trees. If he took the shortcut down the side of the mountain he could cut ten miles off his run. It would be a straight shot down to the highway.

He stood and stared for a second, then took a few steps in that direction. His dad would never know, and every second was precious now. If his dad froze to death when he could have done something to prevent it, he'd never forgive himself. It had been a stupid promise to make.

He tried to ignore the guilt that nagged him as he made his way down to the edge. The wind was rising, the temperature dropping. Snow pelted him every time he stepped out of the trees.

When he reached the edge, he saw that he was much higher than he had thought. The steep, rocky slope looked wet and slippery…but he was still confident that he could do it. He took another step, then stopped.

He couldn't get his father's face out of his mind. *Promise me, Eli.*

Eli sighed deeply and turned back. He had a long way to go if he was going to stay on the road.

Roy Goodner could tell he was in trouble. Despite all the blankets and plastic, he could feel the cold slowly seeping into his body. His face felt frozen and oddly stiff. He was getting sleepy as the warm blood running through his body cooled and slowed down.

He reached for the water bottle, hoping a drink might help wake him up. The water was already half-frozen. He crunched the plastic bottle to break the ice and took two quick swallows—all that would come out.

It didn't matter. Thirst wasn't his main concern right now. He closed his eyes, trying to ignore the cold chills that kept coming in waves, pouring over his body. It must be worse, so much worse, for Eli.

"Lord, let him find help soon," he prayed aloud. His lips were so cold it was hard to form the words.

The blowing snow was stinging Eli's eyes, the gun over his shoulder bumping his back in rhythm with his footfall. When he brushed his hand across his forehead, he found that his hair was stiff with ice.

I wish I had some way to check on Dad, he thought anxiously. It's colder now than it was when I left him. I can feel it.

He pictured his father as he'd seen him last, leaning back in the van's seat, wrapped in plastic from head to toe. Would that be the last time he'd ever see him alive? He quickly shoved away that thought, but others rushed in to replace it—vivid memories that suddenly seemed more real than the snowy landscape around him.

His dad sitting in a 16-foot boat on the lake, teaching Eli how to bait his first hook with a wiggling worm.

His dad using his three-wheeler to "run" from Eli and his little sister, Miriam, as they played chase around the yard.

His dad sitting in the van at baseball games, watching Eli nervously step up to bat—then honking and whistling when he hit the ball.

Thinking back, Eli couldn't remember a time he'd been ashamed of the wheelchair—or his father. It didn't seem to make much difference, his being disabled. Maybe, thought Eli, it was just that his dad didn't let it make a difference.

He had to make it in time to save his father. He just had to.

Eli ran on, darting through the deep shadows cast by the gigantic trees along the road. Several times he heard stirrings in the branches above him. Since the reserve was a known hunting ground for big cats, including 250-pound mountain lions, it made the back of his neck prickle with fear. He shifted the gun from his shoulder back into his hands.

Eyeing the branches overhead, he almost wished his father hadn't spent so much time teaching him about hunting. Unlike African lions, which hunt from the ground, mountain lions are like jaguars—they hunt from the trees, long golden shadows rushing noiselessly from branch to branch. Their prey rarely know they're being stalked until it's too late.

Don't think about it, Eli told himself. Just keep going.

So far he hadn't even seen a deer, much less a lion. Maybe that was a good sign—the lions, bears, wolves and other predators in the reserve had eaten them all and were full. They wouldn't be interested in him.

On the other hand, if all the deer were gone, the larger predators might be starving. When they grew hungry enough, sometimes they'd go after men or even horses. Horses were less than ideal prey, since their kick could kill. Man, however, was soft, pink, and mostly defenseless.

I'm a perfect "to-go" meal, Eli thought wryly. But they'll have to catch me first!

Roy Goodner shivered himself awake, only then realizing he'd fallen asleep. He was shaking so hard that the plastic tarp around him was crackling. He wasn't wearing a watch, but he could tell that several hours had passed.

Mr. Goodner tried to think back over the route they'd taken that morning. How long should it take Eli to run back to the gate? Should he have already been back by now? He was having trouble thinking straight.

I just hope he kept his word and stayed on the road, Mr. Goodner thought. If he tried to cut down that steep slope—he shuddered. All it would take would be one slip, and Eli would be injured and helpless.

A snow-laden branch creaked loudly overhead. Eli spurted forward, hair on end, wondering if the branch had creaked under the weight of a huge padded paw. If so, it wouldn't do much good to run. It might excite a predator to give chase.

He wanted to look behind him, to stop and listen, but he kept going. Every second he wasted would increase the danger to his father.

The afternoon sky was beginning to dim.

I must have come at least six or seven miles by now, he thought helplessly. He kept half-expecting to see a mile-marker sign saying he'd only covered a mile or something. It would fit in with the rest of this day.

His anxiety increased with each step. How long had he been gone? How was his father holding up? He thought again about leaving the road to take the shortcut. His father might have been right about the danger of climbing down from farther up, but now it would be a much shorter climb. It could still cut three or four miles off the trip.

Before he realized what he was doing, he had turned off the trail and was heading straight for the slope.

Dad, you've got to understand, Eli begged silently as he zigzagged through the trees. *I'm doing this for you. I'm afraid I won't make it back to you in time if I stay on the road!* He felt a deep misery that went beyond the cold. Why had this happened to them?

Suddenly, he remembered a time when his dad had used almost those same words. It was the morning Reb, his favorite horse, had died.

Reb had foaled—given birth—several weeks before, and her tiny, beautiful foal still followed her everywhere on its spindly legs. That morning they'd gone out to the pasture to find Reb down on her side, her head crushed by a kick from one of the other horses. The foal was still close by her side, hungry and confused.

"Why did this have to happen?" Mr. Goodner had asked brokenly. Typically, though, he hadn't wasted time complaining. He ran out and bought a nursing bottle and some formula and fed the hungry foal. By the time she was old enough to be weaned from the bottle, she was part of the family.

His father had named her "Promise."

Eli stopped abruptly, feeling like he'd been slapped. Shivering violently, his stomach and legs both in cramps, he suddenly felt like crying. No matter how much he told himself that it would be best if he took the shortcut, that his dad would never know, everything about it felt wrong. He had given his word.

He turned back toward the road. No matter how bad it got, he wouldn't waver again.

Roy Goodner stared at the ceiling of the van, his thoughts bleak. He was shivering so hard now that his teeth chattered. Even the muscles in his shoulders and arms were shaking. Only the lower part of his body remained still.

The sun was going down. He knew he wouldn't last long past nightfall.

He closed his eyes to shut out the numbing cold, but he couldn't shut out his troubling thoughts. Had he allowed Eli to go to his death? This was worse than waking up in the hospital years before to the news that he would be paralyzed for life. This time, it was his son's life which was at stake—and he was helpless to do anything about it.

Take care of Eli, he prayed. *No matter what happens to me, take care of my son.* The bottle of water on the floor beside his seat was now frozen solid.

It was almost four o'clock. Eli kept expecting every bend in the road to lead to the section with the gate. He was exhausted, his legs heavy. He was staggering rather than running now.

Suddenly, from the brush in front of him, a small flock of grouse exploded into the air. Eli jumped and gave a startled exclamation before he realized it was just birds. He was relieved, at least until he thought to wonder what might have frightened them into flight. He hoped it had been him!

A huge shadow fell across the path beside him. Eli looked around wildly, not knowing what he expected to see. Huge grizzlies roamed the area, and Bigfoot stories were common in this part of the country. Maybe it was because they were true, Eli thought in a panic. It would be easy for a Bigfoot to hide in these woods. Panting, he stopped and raised his rifle, squinting through the scope as he turned in a complete circle. Through the rifle's scope, he could see the clear outlines of many odd-shaped trees in the shadows, but no hairy Bigfoot.

He slung the rifle back over his shoulder and ran on.

More time passed. Eli was exhausted. Burning lungs, icy sweat, stitches in his side, a twisting road that never ended…he felt like he was trapped in a nightmare. He rounded another corner and…it was just another long, empty stretch. He was going to go crazy unless this ended soon.

He was looking at the ground when he rounded a corner and finally saw the steel gate. He rushed up and leaned on it, barely able to believe it was real.

"I made it!" he whispered.

He had a hard time fishing the gate key out of his jeans pocket with his cold and swollen hands, and an even harder time fumbling the key into the lock. Leaving the gate open, he dashed forward onto the pavement, hoping to flag down a car.

The highway was empty in both directions. It figured. Not much had gone right so far that day.

Eli hesitated, trying to decide which way to go. He couldn't see houses in either direction. He turned one way and ran a few steps, then stopped. Somehow, it didn't feel right. He turned around and ran in the other direction.

Almost a half-mile later, Eli was beginning to think he'd made the wrong choice when he spotted a small log cabin just ahead. A pickup truck was parked in the driveway, and an old man was outside working in the garage.

He stumbled up the driveway. "Sir!" he shouted hoarsely. "May I use your phone?"

The man spun around, obviously startled. "Stop right there!" he yelled suspiciously. "And drop the gun!"

Eli looked down at the rifle in his hands. After running with it for almost five hours, he'd forgotten all about it. "Okay," he said, "but I need help! My dad is stranded way up in the reserve. He's crippled, and he's going to freeze to death if I don't get him out of there soon."

The man studied Eli for a moment, then nodded. "Put your gun in my truck, then come on inside."

Eli almost threw the rifle into the cab. Inside the log cabin, the air was so warm that it hurt. Eli had been cold for far too long.

"Phone's over there," the man said, pointing.

Punching in the number with still-numb fingers, Eli hoped his mom would answer on the first ring. She was much closer than the nearest ambulance service.

The sun was going down. They needed to act fast.

No answer.

He tried several times, getting more and more frustrated. Finally he slammed down the phone. "My mom's not home," he explained. Even to his own ears, his voice sounded desperate.

"Hm," the old man said thoughtfully. "You know, I've got a neighbor who volunteers with a mountain search and rescue group. He's got a four wheel drive ambulance. If he's in town...."

"How far off is he?"

"Just over two miles. I'll call him for you."

Eli listened anxiously. He was starting to worry that the neighbor wasn't home either when the old man spoke. "Hi, it's Will Rogers. I've got a young man here who's needing some help bringing his father down off the mountain. Sounds like he's up Eagle Creek Road somewhere." He listened for a second. "Yeah, I'd appreciate it. Thanks."

He hung up the phone and turned to Eli. "He'll be here in a second."

Eli couldn't believe it. The first person he'd stumbled across just *happened* to know a mountain search and rescue worker? After the way everything else had gone that day, it seemed almost too easy.

"Thanks," he said sincerely. "Thanks a lot."

He paced restlessly, watching night fall as he waited. Ten minutes later a Prichard Search and Rescue ambulance pulled up. Eli said a hasty goodbye to Mr.

Rogers, then ran out and climbed in beside the ambulance driver.

"Back that way," he said, pointing. "I left the gate unlocked."

It was almost dark now, and the temperature outside had dropped well below zero. As the ambulance raced up the dirt road, covering ground in minutes that had taken Eli a half-hour to run, he worried about his father.

Please let everything turn out okay, he silently prayed. *Help him hang on until we get there.*

As they got closer to the turnoff, Eli perched on the edge of his seat straining to see through the gloom. What if it was too dark to see his orange cap? He wasn't sure he could pick out the right trail without it.

He was starting to worry that they'd passed it already in the dark when he spotted it. "Right there!" he shouted, pointing. "That's it!"

The ambulance driver looked doubtfully at the muddy and brush-covered trail. "I'm not sure these tires will make it through that. It won't do your dad any good for us to get two vehicles stuck in here. We'll have to go the rest of the way on foot."

Eli was immediately out the door and running. Now that they were so close, all his worst fears rushed to the surface. What if his dad was dead? What would he do? It was too much to handle.

He saw the brush patch ahead and plowed into it, recklessly shoving the sharp branches aside. "Dad!" he yelled. "Dad, are you okay?"

Silence. Eli reached the van and tugged at the door. It was too dark to see anything inside. "Dad! Are you okay?" he yelled again. He jerked the door open.

His father was still wrapped from head to toe in the tarp, but his face looked sheet-white, frozen. Then, very slowly, Mr. Goodner turned his head. "I'm okay," he said faintly, his lips barely moving.

Eli let out a frosty breath, feeling weak with relief. "Cold?" he asked, just to have something to say. He'd been so afraid he'd never hear his father's voice again.

"Yeah, pretty cold."

"I thought you'd be a popsicle."

Mr. Goodner smiled weakly at the joke. "I'm tough."

The ambulance driver finally caught up with Eli. "I'm glad to see your dad's all right," he said with obvious relief. "Let's get him out of here and into the ambulance."

Working quickly, they helped Mr. Goodner into his wheelchair and half carried him out of the brush. They pushed him back up the trail in his chair, tilting it back in a "wheelie" so they could move faster.

When they reached the ambulance, though, Mr. Goodner asked if he could sit up front instead of riding on a bed in the back. "I had enough of ambulances and hospital beds back when I had my accident," he explained. "Besides, I'll be closer to the heat vents up front."

"Whatever you want, sir," the driver said.

Eli plopped down to sit on the floor between the two front seats. He still felt a little stunned. It was hard to believe it was all over.

After a moment his dad looked down at him with an odd expression. "Did you stay on the road like you promised, Eli?"

Eli nodded. "But I could've been back here hours ago if I'd cut down the slope. I had to run nearly fourteen miles just to get back to the gate!"

"I told you it was farther than you thought." Mr. Goodner paused to let a violent wave of shivering pass. "I knew it would take longer, but I was more worried about you hurting yourself. I couldn't have done anything to help you."

The driver started the ambulance and turned on the heater. Mr. Goodner leaned forward into the blast of warm air, eyes closed, soaking it up.

"Eli, I'm glad you kept your promise," he said softly.

The blood was already coming back to his cheeks and fingers as the ambulance went bumping down the mountain into the icy night, the new snow dusting the windshield.

Roy Goodner was treated for hypothermia and quickly recovered.

Eli Goodner received a Heroism Award for "demonstrating heroism and skill in saving or attempting to save a life" from the Boy Scouts of America, and also a Heroism Award for Meritorious Action from the National Court of Honor.

Eli, Roy and Sherrie Goodner

Turn the page for a sneak preview of

Real Kids Real Adventures #12:

Train Track Rescue

by Deborah Morris

A California teen has only seconds to act when a train bears down on two young neighbor children... two brothers are marking a field for their father when his crop-dusting plane strikes a power line and crashes before their eyes...a twelve-year-old girl puts her Red Cross babysitting training to the test when a toddler is discovered at the bottom of a backyard pool. More action-packed stories about real kids just like *you!*

Look for this latest volume in the *Real Kids Real Adventures* series.

Train Track Rescue

The Joe Terry Story

"**H**e doesn't have a pulse!"

Joe Terry looked up anxiously, his fingers lightly touching the small boy's neck. Beside him, an adult paramedic leaned over another victim.

"You know what to do, Joe!" the paramedic barked. "Start CPR!"

Joe ran a hand through his short brown hair, trying to quickly organize his thoughts. Growing up, he had often daydreamed about having the chance to save somebody's life. Now, at age sixteen, he was being put to the test.

Placing one hand on the boy's forehead and the other under his chin, Joe gently tilted the child's head back and pinched his nose closed. Then he leaned down and covered the small mouth with his own, trying to form a tight seal. The boy's skin was cold and stiff, but Joe tried not to think about it. He gently breathed into the boy's mouth, watching to make sure the air went in.

Good, he thought when he saw the small chest move. I'm doing it right. He came up for a quick gulp of air, then leaned down to give the child a second breath. He was relieved to see the chest move again. It was working!

Now for chest compressions. The boy wasn't breathing, and his heart wasn't beating. Joe knew that without oxygen, a brain will start to die within minutes. He needed to force the boy's heart to pump the oxygen through his body. If he did it wrong…

"You're doing fine," the paramedic said crisply from somewhere over his shoulder. "Keep it up."

Joe didn't look up. Keeping his brown eyes fixed on the small body, he placed the heel of one hand on the center of the boy's chest and began to press. "ONE and TWO and THREE and FOUR and FIVE!" he counted aloud with each compression. By the time he reached "five" he was a little breathless from the effort. He paused to give the child another slow breath.

"Keep going!" the paramedic urged.

Joe repeated the cycle several times: five compressions, one breath, five compressions, one breath. After about a minute, he stopped to recheck the boy's pulse and breathing. He placed his fingers lightly on the boy's neck and leaned his ear close to his mouth to listen for breathing. He didn't have much hope of hearing anything, but he couldn't give up. The boy looked like he was only four or five years old.

Joe felt a hand grasp his shoulder. "Okay, Joe, I

think you've done all you can." It was the paramedic, Kevin Daniels. He added sorrowfully, "I'm afraid this one's not going to make it. Go ahead and rip out his lungs."

All twenty of the Merced County Sheriff's Explorers burst out laughing, breaking the tension in the room. Joe joined in, shaking his head. Kevin Daniels, their CPR instructor, loved to joke around. Joe reached down and awkwardly yanked on the clear plastic sticking out of the little boy's mouth. The manikin's "lungs"—a long plastic bag—pulled all the way out. Joe tore off the used lungs at the perforation and got the manikin ready for the next Explorer.

At the end of the class, as the other teens spilled out into the bright weekend sun, Joe stayed behind to talk to Kevin. He grinned as he looked around the near empty classroom. With all the little dummies still sprawled on the floor, it looked like a major disaster scene.

"I just wanted to say thanks," Joe said self-consciously. "You're a good instructor."

Kevin smiled and slapped him on the back. "And you're a good student," he said. "You'll make a fine law enforcement officer one day."

Dear Reader,

Have you heard or read about someone who should be a "Real Kid"?

Here's what it takes to be a "Real Kids" story:

1. It has to be TRUE. All the stories in *Real Kids Real Adventures* are told just as they happened. I can't use made-up stories, no matter how exciting they are.

2. It has to INVOLVE KIDS between the ages of 8 and 17. Younger kids and adults can be involved, but the main characters must be kids and teens.

3. It has to be DRAMATIC. *Real Kids Real Adventures* is about kids who are heroes or survivors, not about things like diseases or child abuse.

4. It has to have happened IN THE LAST THREE YEARS. It can take a year (or more) for a book to be published or a TV episode to be filmed. We'd like the kids to still be kids when their stories come out!

5. It has to have a HAPPY ENDING!

If you find a story, send me a newspaper clipping or other information to help me track it down. If I'm able to use it (and if you are the first one to tell me about that particular story) I'll print your name in the book and send you a free autographed copy when it comes out.

Let me know what you think of this volume of *Real Kids Real Adventures*. You can write to me at: P.O. Box 461572, Garland, TX 75046-1572, or email me at deb@realkids.com.

Deborah Morris